Karen's

Look for these
and other books about Karen
in the
Baby-sitters Little Sister series

Little Sister

Karen's Softball Mystery
Ann M. Martin

Illustrations by Susan Tang

A
LITTLE APPLE
PAPERBACK

SCHOLASTIC INC.
New York Toronto London Auckland Sydney

*The author gratefully acknowledges
Stephanie Calmenson
for her help
with this book.*

No part of this publication may be reproduced in whole or in part, or stored in a retrieval system, or transmitted in any form or by any means, electronic, mechanical, photocopying, recording, or otherwise, without written permission of the publisher. For information regarding permission, write to Scholastic Inc., 555 Broadway, New York, NY 10012.

ISBN 0-590-26214-9

12 11 10 9 8 7 6 5 4 3 2 1   6 7 8 9/9 0 1/0

Printed in the U.S.A.   40

First Scholastic printing, June 1996

Up in the Treehouse

"You carry the cookies, Andrew. Try not to drop them, okay?" I said.

It was a warm, sunny Wednesday in June. I was about to have an after-school snack in the treehouse with my little brother Andrew. He is four going on five.

Andrew and I built the treehouse with our little-house friends. (We have two houses — a big house and a little house. I will tell you more about them later.) Everyone gets to use the treehouse. But Andrew and I are lucky because it is right in our backyard.

I was on the top step when I heard something drop.

"Oops," said Andrew.

I turned around and saw the bag of cookies on the ground. Andrew looked as though he were going to cry.

"It is all right," I said. "Cookies taste good even when they are in little pieces."

I thought that was a very grown-up thing to say. Especially for someone like me who is only seven.

My name is Karen Brewer. I have blonde hair, blue eyes, and a bunch of freckles. Oh, yes. I wear glasses. I have two pairs. I wear my blue pair for reading. I wear my pink pair the rest of the time. And I do not mind eating crumbled cookies.

Andrew got the cookies and we put them on a plate. (Really we needed a bowl. They looked more like cereal now than cookies.) I poured us each a cup of apple juice.

"I am glad we are not having Swiss cheese today," I said.

"What is wrong with Swiss cheese?" asked Andrew.

"If you eat Swiss cheese you can get holes in your knees!" I replied.

Andrew thought this was hysterically funny. I sang him the silly Swiss cheese song my teacher, Mrs. Hoffman, taught us at school.

I am in second grade at Stoneybrook Academy here in Stoneybrook, Connecticut. Mrs. Hoffman is my substitute teacher. I used to call her Hatey Hoffman. But she turned out to be really nice. Even so, I could hardly wait for my real teacher, Ms. Colman, to come back. Ms. Colman went away to take care of her brand-new baby, Jane. I missed Ms. Colman a lot.

"You could not run very well if you had holes in your knees," said Andrew.

"Huh?" I said. I was not listening to Andrew. I was busy thinking about Ms. Colman and her new baby.

4

"I said it would be hard to run with holes in your knees," Andrew repeated. "Kristy would not like that."

Kristy is our stepsister. She is thirteen and the best stepsister in the whole world. She is also our softball coach. She started a softball team called Kristy's Krushers.

"I think we have a practice tomorrow," I said. "I will call Kristy later to find out."

Kristy lives at the big house. Big house. Little house. Do you want to know why I have two houses? I will tell you.

Hello, Is Kristy There?

A long time ago when I was little I lived in one big house with Mommy, Daddy, and Andrew. Then things started changing. Mommy and Daddy started to fight a lot. They told Andrew and me that they loved us very much. But they just could not get along with each other anymore. So they got divorced.

Mommy moved with Andrew and me to a little house not too far away in Stoneybrook. That is when she met Seth. Mommy and Seth got married. That is how Seth became my stepfather. Now Mommy, Seth, Andrew, and I live at the little house. There are pets, too. They are Midgie, Seth's dog; Rocky, Seth's cat; Emily Junior, my pet rat; and Bob, Andrew's hermit crab.

Daddy stayed at the big house after the divorce. (It is the house he grew up in.) He met Elizabeth. They got married and Elizabeth became my stepmother.

Elizabeth was married once before and has four children. One of them is Kristy. The others are my stepbrothers. They are David Michael, who is seven like me, and Sam and Charlie, who are so old they are in high school.

I have an adopted sister at the big house. Her name is Emily Michelle. Emily is two and a half. She was adopted from a faraway country called Vietnam. I love her a lot. (That is why I named my pet rat after her.)

One more person lives at the big house. That is Nannie. She is Elizabeth's mother. That makes her my stepgrandmother. She came to help take care of Emily. But really she helps take care of everyone.

There are also pets at the big house. They are Shannon, who is David Michael's big Bernese mountain dog puppy; Boo-Boo, who is Daddy's cranky old cat; Crystal Light the Second, who is my goldfish; and Goldfishie, who is Andrew's caterpillar. (Did I fool you?)

Andrew and I switch houses every month — one month we live at the little house, the next month at the big house. (Emily Junior and Bob go with us.)

I have special names for my brother and me. I call us Andrew Two-Two and Karen Two-Two. (I thought up those names after my teacher read a book to our class. It was called *Jacob Two-Two Meets the Hooded Fang*.) I call us those names because we have two of so many things. We have two mommies and two daddies, two houses and two families, two cats and two dogs. We each have two sets of toys and clothes and books — one set at each house. I have two bicycles.

Andrew has two tricycles. I have two stuffed cats. (Goosie lives at the little house. Moosie lives at the big house.) I even have two best friends. Nancy Dawes lives next door to Mommy's house. Hannie Papadakis lives across the street and one house down from Daddy's house. (Nancy and Hannie and I call ourselves the Three Musketeers.)

Andrew and I had finished our treehouse snack. It was time to call Kristy. I went into the little house and dialed the number for the big house.

I listened to it ring once, twice . . .

Phone Calls

Kristy picked up the phone.

"Hello," she said.

"Hi, it's me, Karen," I replied. "I forgot what time practice is tomorrow."

Kristy told me that practice was going to be at four o'clock. That was good. Andrew and I would have time to come home for our after-school snack and change into our softball shirts. Everyone on the team has a shirt that says Kristy's Krushers. Only my shirt says Crushers with a C instead of a K. I like it that way because Crushers is supposed to be spelled with a C. I know that because I am an excellent speller.

After our snack Mommy would drive us over to Stoneybrook Elementary School. That is where our practices are usually held.

Kristy and I talked for awhile. She caught me up on the latest Krusher news.

"I cannot believe how many kids want to join the team this year," she said. "It's a real spring rush. You better be ready for a hectic day tomorrow."

"No problem," I replied.

I love hectic days. They are my favorite kind.

When I finished talking to Kristy, I asked to speak to David Michael. (I also love talking on the phone.)

"I'm sorry, Karen," said Kristy. "David Michael is not allowed to come to the phone. He has been having some trouble in school lately. My mom is being very strict with him. It is his homework time now. I am not allowed to disturb him."

Hmm. This was something new.

"Excuse me, Karen, I would like to make a call when you are finished," said Mommy.

I wanted to speak to everyone at the big house. But I did not want to tie up the phone any longer.

"See you at practice tomorrow!" I said to Kristy.

As soon as I hung up, the phone rang. It was Nancy.

"Hi, Nancy!" I said.

Mommy gave me a please-hurry-up look.

I held up one finger. That meant one minute. That seemed an awfully short time to talk to my friend. So I held up one more finger.

Nancy reminded me of some very exciting news.

"Do you realize that Ms. Colman is coming back to school on *Monday*?" she said. "That is just five days away!"

Wow. The time with Mrs. Hoffman had passed by quickly.

12

"We should do something special on Monday," I said. "We should have a welcome-back party for Ms. Colman."

Nancy thought this was a great idea. We decided to talk to Mrs. Hoffman about it as soon as we got to school the next day.

I hung up the phone and looked at Mommy. She smiled.

"Three and a half minutes," she said. "That was not bad at all."

4

Party Plans

"Addie, would you take attendance, please?" asked Mrs. Hoffman.

Bullfrogs! It was Thursday morning. Mrs. Hoffman had just come into the classroom. I wished she had called on me. I like doing important jobs such as taking attendance. (Oh, well. Addie Sidney is really nice. So I did not mind too much.)

Mrs. Hoffman passed the attendance book to Addie. Addie rested it on the tray of her wheelchair and began checking off names. She looked my way first and smiled. (You see. I told you Addie is nice.) I smiled back. Addie put a check in the book.

Then she looked across my row. I sit at the very front with Natalie Springer and Ricky Torres. (Ricky is my pretend husband. We got married on the playground at recess one day.) The three of us are in front because we wear glasses. Ms. Colman said we could see better this way. (Ms. Colman wears glasses, too.)

Addie put two more checks in the book. I looked around the room as if I were taking attendance with her. I saw Pamela Harding. (She is my best enemy.) She was passing notes to Jannie Gilbert and Leslie Morris. The three of them are best friends like the Three Musketeers. Only we were best friends first.

I saw Bobby Gianelli. He lives on my street and helped build the treehouse. (He used to be a bully, but now he is nice most of the time.)

Terri and Tammy Barkan, who are twins,

15

were there. Audrey Green, Hank Reubens, Omar Harris, and Chris Lamar were there.

And, of course, Hannie and Nancy were there. I waved to them. (I used to sit in the back with them before I got my glasses.) They waved back.

Addie finished taking the real attendance and I finished taking my make-believe attendance at the same time. (Two kids were out sick.)

Addie handed the book back to Mrs. Hoffman. I raised my hand. When Mrs. Hoffman called on me I told her my gigundoly good idea.

"Ms. Colman is coming back on Monday. I think we should have a welcome-back party for her. Do you think the class could plan it together?"

"It sounds like a wonderful idea to me. We'll take a class vote," said Mrs. Hoffman. "Anyone who would like to plan a party for Ms. Colman, raise your hand."

Every hand in the room popped up.

"It is unanimous," said Mrs. Hoffman.

"If you like, I will come in on Monday to help with the party."

That gave me a second idea. I wanted to pass a note to Hannie and Nancy telling them what it was. But I was afraid Mrs. Hoffman would see it. That would be terrible because the idea was about her.

I waited until recess. Then I gathered my classmates around me and told everyone all together.

"I think we should have two parties at once," I said. "We can have a welcome-back party for Ms. Colman. And we can have a good-bye party for Mrs. Hoffman. We can surprise both of them."

We took another vote. It was unanimous again. I spent the rest of recess planning the party with my classmates. We made sure Mrs. Hoffman could not hear us. We wanted her party to be a big surprise.

Too Many Players

That afternoon Mommy drove Andrew, me, and Nancy to our first softball practice of the season. (Nancy does not like to play very much. But she comes to help Kristy with the equipment.)

"Hi, Karen! Hi, Nancy," called Hannie when we got to the field. "Can you believe how many kids showed up for practice?"

"Wow!" I said. "There sure are a *lot*. I guess being a Krusher is cool this year."

The team is made up of kids who don't play in Little League or T-Ball. There are

18

usually about twenty players. I went around saying hi to some of the regulars. I said hi to Nicky Pike, who is eight, and is one of the two main pitchers (David Michael is the other); Haley Braddock, who is nine, and is one of the Krushers cheerleaders; Matthew Braddock, her brother, who is seven, and is one of the best players on the team (we talk to him in sign language because he is deaf).

There were other kids I wanted to say hi to, but Kristy was calling for our attention. We gathered around to hear what our coach had to say.

"I am glad that so many of you want to join the Krushers this year," said Kristy. "Right now it looks as though there may be too many kids for one team and not enough for two teams. For the first time in Krushers history, we may have to make some cuts."

"Boo! No way!" called the kids.

"I said we *may* have to make cuts," replied Kristy. "We are not doing it yet.

Everyone will get to play ball today."

"Hooray! Yea!" called the kids.

Practice was off to an interesting start.

"I'm going to divide you up into two teams. I want you to step lively and show each other what it means to be a Krusher," said Kristy. "Are Krushers lazy?"

"No way!" we all replied.

"Are Krushers bad sports?" she asked.

"No way!" we all replied.

"Do Krushers know how to win?" she asked.

"Yes! Go Krushers!" we shouted.

Just then a boy and a girl I had never seen before walked onto the field. The girl had long dark hair and was wearing cool clothes. She looked about twelve. The boy was tagging along behind. He was not as cool. He looked about eight. The girl stepped up to Kristy and introduced herself.

"Hi, I'm Barbie Spencer and this is my brother Julian," she said. "Julian is here to play ball." She lowered her voice a little. I moved in closer to hear what she was saying.

"We're new in town and Julian is kind of shy," said Barbie. "I thought if he joined the team he might make some new friends."

"You're right. He will make lots of friends here," said Kristy. "Come on, Julian. We are just about ready to start the practice."

Barbie sat on the grass with the parents, baby-sitters, and other big brothers and sisters of the players.

"Okay, everyone," said Kristy. "I want you to show me what you've got. We have a big game coming up against Bart's Bashers to celebrate the beginning of summer. It is going to be held as soon as school is out. That is just a few weeks away."

She divided us up into two teams. With so many kids, it took forever to get called to bat. We bumped into each other in the

outfield. And the regular players argued with the new players.

By the end of the game everyone was gigundoly grumpy, and I was gigundoly happy to go home.

A Practice Game

The Bashers showed up at the ballfield just after we arrived on Saturday. Bart and Kristy, the two team coaches, had agreed to have a practice game. (Bart Taylor is in Kristy's grade at school.)

"Nicky, you are our only pitcher today," said Kristy.

"Where is David Michael?" I asked. "Is he okay?"

"He was not allowed to come. He had to stay home to catch up on his schoolwork," replied Kristy. "He was really mad about that."

I would be, too, I thought.

Kristy gathered us around for a pep talk.

"Who are we going to play today?" she asked.

"The Bashers!" we replied.

"And who are we going to beat today?" she asked.

"The Bashers!" we replied.

(We did not believe it, though. The Bashers are a little older than the Krushers. So they usually win.)

The Krushers were at bat first. Kristy lined us up in alphabetical order. With a B for Brewer, I was one of the first.

"Keep your eye on the ball, Karen," said Kristy.

"I will," I replied.

I kept my eye on the ball. I watched it go right by me. I watched the second ball sail by, too.

"All you have to do is concentrate," said Kristy.

No, all I have to do is hit it, I thought. You know what? I did! I hit the ball! I ran like the wind and made it to first base. The kids cheered for me and I took a bow.

A kid named Marty Benson was next. He is a second-grader at Stoneybrook Elementary School.

"Atta boy, Marty!" called a man wearing dark glasses.

"Who is that?" I asked Julie Rich, the Bashers' first base player.

"He's Marty's dad," replied Julie. "He wants Marty to hit a home run every time he gets up to bat."

"That is hard to do," I said.

Marty swung at the first pitch and missed. He swung and hit the second pitch. But it was a foul.

"It's now or never, Marty!" called Mr. Benson.

Marty swung at the third pitch and missed again. He looked very disappointed.

"That bat must be no good," shouted Mr. Benson, running to Kristy.

"We use perfectly good bats, Mr. Benson," Kristy replied. "Sometimes kids miss. And that's okay."

"I think you need to be a little tougher on these kids," said a guy who looked about as old as Sam and Charlie.

"Excuse me?" said Kristy. "Who are you?"

"I am Jack Darvin. My sister, Alice, is new on your team. She's eight. I want her looking good when she comes up to bat," said Jack.

"She will look as good as she looks," replied Kristy.

"If you ask me, you are going about this all wrong. You should not put the kids up to bat in alphabetical order. You should put the best players up first," said Jack.

"Well, I did not ask you," said Kristy. "Batter up!"

When it was Alice's turn, she walked up

to home plate and waited for the ball to come her way.

"Time out!" called Jack.

"Excuse me!" said Kristy. "I am the coach. I am the only one who calls for a time out."

"Someone needs to show my sister how to hold the bat correctly," said Jack. "Helping her out is your job. But since you are not doing it, I will."

Kristy gave Jack a meanie-mo look.

"Play ball!" she called.

Alice tried her best, but struck out. Jack stamped his foot on the ground. The next player struck out also. By the time the game was over, the score was Bashers 6, Krushers 0.

Well, at least I made it to first base.

Krushers-Only

Some Krushers did not get a chance to play on Saturday. That is because there were so many of us. Kristy called for a Krushers-only practice on Sunday. She split us into two teams.

David Michael was pitching for one team. (He finished all his homework on Saturday, so he was allowed to come to practice again.) Nicky was pitching for the other team.

Natalie Springer was first at bat. I did not think she would get a hit. She is not such a good ball player. That is partly because her socks are always drooping. She stops to pull them up at the oddest times. I once saw the ball fly past her and she didn't even know because she was bending down!

"Natalie, are your socks okay?" asked Kristy.

Natalie looked down. Her socks were bunched around her ankles. She bent over and pulled them up.

"Play ball!" called Kristy.

Nicky threw the ball.

Whack! Natalie hit the very first pitch! She got all the way to second base.

"Way to go, Natalie!" we all shouted.

David Michael was up next. He looked unhappy.

"Has anyone seen my bat?" he asked.

"It should be with the others," said Nancy. "I know we brought it."

"It isn't there. I already looked," replied David Michael.

We stopped the game to look for David Michael's bat. It was taking forever.

Finally Kristy said, "We cannot spend our whole practice looking for your bat, David Michael. It is no surprise that it is missing. You have been *so* sloppy and disorganized lately."

David Michael looked hurt. I felt bad for him. I picked up the bat I had used the day before.

"Here, try this one," I said. "I used it yesterday and got to first base. It is a very good bat."

David Michael used the bat. He struck out.

Our next two players struck out, too. (Natalie was disappointed because she did not get to run to home plate.)

It was the other team's turn at bat. Hannie was first up.

"Has anyone seen a batting glove?" she asked.

"Here is one," said Kristy.

"No, that is a left-hand batting glove. I need a right-hand glove," replied Hannie.

"I saw someone else use one today. So

it must be here somewhere," said Kristy.

We looked and looked, but could not find it. (We did find David Michael's bat, though. It was under somebody's sweatshirt.)

"Can you please play without the glove, Hannie?" asked Kristy. She seemed annoyed about all the missing equipment.

"I guess so," replied Hannie. She seemed annoyed, too. She was even more annoyed when she struck out.

It was another hectic practice. Things were missing. Our coach was cranky. Players were striking out (even more than usual). At least I did not strike out. That was because I never made it up to bat.

I did not mind too much about the practice, though. I had other important things on my mind. I had a lot to do when I got home.

I had to pick out a special outfit to wear to school on Monday. I had to help Mommy frost the cupcakes we had made the night before. And I had to make two cards — one for Ms. Colman and one for Mrs. Hoffman.

I had to do all these things because Monday was Mrs. Hoffman's last day as our substitute teacher. And it was Ms. Colman's first day back. Hooray!

Ms. Colman, Where Are You?

On Monday morning, Nancy and I waited for the school bus together.

"You look very pretty," I said. Nancy was all dressed up for the party.

"Thank you. So do you," Nancy replied.

I was hoping she would say that. I had on a new green jumper with a yellow T-shirt underneath. I had on yellow socks and a yellow ribbon in my hair. I had even tied a yellow ribbon around the box of frosted cupcakes I was carrying. (Nancy was bringing berries and melon slices for the party.)

All we could talk about on the way to school was Ms. Colman and the party.

"I cannot wait to see her," I said. "I wonder if she will look different."

"Maybe she will look tired," replied Nancy. "Some little babies cry a lot at night. I know because of Danny." (Danny is Nancy's baby brother.)

"I hope Ms. Colman brings pictures of Jane," I said.

I hoped there would be one of Jane wrapped up in the baby present I gave her. It was a beautiful blanket I knitted all by myself. (Well, almost all by myself. Nannie helped a little.)

Nancy and I were the first ones off the bus when it pulled up at school.

"Let's hurry," I said. "Ms. Colman may have come in early. We do not want her sitting all alone."

We ran into school. We were not as fast as usual because we were carrying our cupcakes and fruit.

We stopped at Mr. Berger's class, which

is right next door to ours. (We had arranged to leave our party things in his room so the surprise would not be ruined.)

When I got to our door, I stopped short. Someone was sitting at Ms. Colman's desk. But it was not Ms. Colman. It was Mrs. Hoffman. I burst through the door.

"Hurry, Mrs. Hoffman! You need to hide!" I said. "If Ms. Colman comes in and sees you, the surprise will be ruined."

"I am sorry, Karen. But there is not going to be a surprise for Ms. Colman today. She is not coming in after all," Ms. Hoffman replied.

"Why not? Where is she?" I asked.

"Ms. Colman is at home. I know how much you wanted her to be here. But she is not quite ready to leave Jane and come back to school," said Mrs. Hoffman.

I felt my shoulders droop.

"When *will* she be ready?" I asked.

"She has promised to come back for the final week of school. It is not very far off," said Mrs. Hoffman.

More kids started coming into the room.

"What's up?" asked Hannie. "Where is Ms. Colman?"

Nancy and I told everyone the news as they arrived.

"You see," said Natalie. "I told you so."

Natalie is a big worrier. The day Ms. Colman told us that she was going to take a leave from school, Natalie started worrying that she might never come back at all.

Hmm. I was starting to wonder if Natalie had been right.

I was feeling kind of gloomy and wondering what we were going to do with all our party food when Mrs. Hoffman made an announcement.

"I know Ms. Colman cares about you very much. I am sure she would not want you to feel sad today," said Mrs. Hoffman. "So I think we should go ahead with our party this afternoon. It will not be a welcome-back party. It will be a see-you-soon party."

We all thought this was a gigundoly good idea. Hooray for Mrs. Hoffman!

Very Mysterious

There was another Krushers practice after school that day. Kristy was calling for practices almost every day. It was the only way to give everyone a chance to play.

Kristy divided us up into two teams. (She changed the teams each time we played.) Nicky had a dentist appointment, so we needed another pitcher.

Kristy got her notebook from the equipment bag and began leafing through it. I looked over her shoulder. Kristy's notes about the players are in the book. She writes down statistics and things like that.

"This is strange," she said. "Some pages are missing."

"Maybe they fell into the equipment bag," said Nancy.

"No way. The pages could not have fallen out by themselves," Kristy replied. "They had to be ripped out. But we cannot do anything about it now."

She turned to Matt and asked him in sign language if he would fill in as pitcher. Kristy knows she can count on Matt to play any position because he is so good.

"Ricky, you are first at bat for your team," she said.

"Go, Ricky!" I called. (I always cheer for my pretend husband no matter which team he is on.)

David Michael was already on the pitcher's mound. The rest of us took our positions. (I was way out in the field with a bunch of other kids. Boring!)

"Play ball!" called Kristy.

First came the wind-up. Then the pitch.

Wham! Ricky hit the ball down the third base line.

"Go, Ricky!" I shouted. Ricky made it to second and stopped.

Then Hannie, who was the catcher, called time out. I heard her tell Kristy she had to go to the bathroom.

"Natalie, will you fill in as catcher?" asked Kristy.

"Sure," Natalie replied. "But I need the left-hand catcher's mitt."

"Nancy, have you seen it?" called Kristy.

"It was right here on top of the equipment bag when we started. But I do not see it now," Nancy replied.

Uh-oh. Missing pages. Missing catcher's mitt.

"Let's not waste time looking for it now," said Kristy. "Natalie, you can be catcher another day. Karen, will you fill in?"

Yes! I took my place behind home plate.

"Play ball!" I called. Kristy gave me a Look. (It is not the catcher's job to start the game.)

42

Jackie Rodowsky was up next. First he tripped on his way to home plate. (Jackie has a lot of accidents.) Then he got three strikes in a row.

It was time for the teams to switch places. Matt headed for the pitcher's mound. He picked up a ball. A grossed-out look spread across his face.

"Slimy and sticky!" he signed.

A few of us ran over to check it out. The ball was covered with sticky white paste. It took a while, but we figured out that it was Elmer's glue.

Things were getting *very* mysterious.

Detectives

More things were stolen at practice on Tuesday: two bats, another left-hand catcher's mitt, another right-hand batting glove. On Wednesday, Kristy's notebook disappeared for awhile. When it turned up again, something mysterious had happened to it.

"I don't get it. Someone erased my statistics and wrote in phony numbers," said Kristy.

Who was doing these mysterious things? And why? This was a case for serious detectives. It was a case for the Three Musketeers.

I called Hannie and Nancy over for a meeting.

"We have a real mystery here," I said. "If we do not solve the case soon, the Krushers could be ruined for the season."

"You are right," said Nancy. "I will watch the equipment very carefully. No one will get near it without my seeing."

"I will watch to make sure no one gets Kristy's notebook again," said Hannie.

"I will be a secret spy," I said. "If anyone is plotting against the Krushers, I will hear them!"

(I am not allowed to spy at home. But this was different. Spying is important when you are working on a case.)

"Come on, Karen!" called Kristy. "I want you to be catcher again today."

"Great," I whispered to my friends. "I will be behind home plate. It is the perfect place for a spy."

When I got to my position, Paul Johnson, one of the new kids on the team, was arguing with Kristy.

"Karen was catcher yesterday," said Paul. "Just because she is your sister does not mean she gets to be catcher every time."

"I am letting her be catcher again because she did a good job yesterday," said Kristy.

"I am a good catcher, too," moaned Paul. "When do I get a turn?"

"And how about Alice?" said her big brother, Jack. "She is a good catcher. You have to give her a turn."

"Oh, all right," said Kristy. "Paul and Alice can replace Karen and Ricky as catchers when the game is half over."

Boo. I felt like saying something to whiny Paul and pushy Jack. But I decided that I could spy just as well from the outfield. Maybe even better because there were so many players out there.

Once Kristy got the teams set up, she called, "Play ball!"

Hannie was up at bat first.

"Psst! Have you seen anything suspicious?" I asked.

"Not yet," whispered Hannie.

Matt pitched a perfect fly ball to Hannie. Thwack! Hannie hit it. She was safe at first base.

"Way to go, Hannie!" I called, even though she is on the other team. (The Three Musketeers stick together. One for all and all for one.)

Behind me I heard familiar voices. I turned for a second and saw Jerry and Joanna. They are Bashers. Hmm. What were they doing here? Maybe they were spying on the Krushers. Maybe they were trying to get important information to give to the Bashers. Information that could help them win the big game.

Things were getting exciting. As soon as the inning was over, I reported the news to Hannie and Nancy.

Interesting Clues

On Thursday, Kristy asked Matt to pitch again.

"Where is David Michael?" I asked.

"He had more schoolwork to do," replied Kristy. "Mom and Watson are being really strict with him. They say schoolwork is more important than softball."

Poor David Michael. Who wants to stay inside on a sunny day when everyone else is practicing softball?

Not David Michael. About fifteen minutes into the practice he showed up.

"Hi! Did you finish your schoolwork?" I asked.

"Not yet. But I *really* want to play. I snuck out," replied David Michael.

"I heard that," said Kristy. "You are not staying here. No way. You have to go home right this minute."

"You are always siding with Mom and Watson. You never take *my* side," yelled David Michael. He gave Kristy a dirty look and stomped off.

Before the game started, the Three Musketeers Detective Agency had a meeting. (We decided to call ourselves that name until the case was solved.)

"I noticed something interesting," said Hannie. "Only left-hand catcher's mitts and right-hand batting gloves have been taken. That means if the thief is keeping them, he or she must be right-handed."

"Excellent," I said. "Now we have to find out who is right-handed and who is left-handed."

"How will we do it?" asked Nancy.

"We can study the kids who are playing," said Hannie. "And we can toss balls to the other kids and see which hand they catch with."

We started doing our research right away. By the time Kristy called for a break, we had learned that most kids were right-handed. There seemed to be only a few left-handers: Natalie, Julian, Marty, and two new kids, Margaret and Allen. We still had more testing to do. Then I had a brainstorm.

"I think we are on the wrong track," I said. "Everyone is allowed to use Krushers equipment. You do not need your own. That means no one would have to steal it to use it."

"So why is equipment disappearing?" asked Nancy.

I had to think hard.

"I've got it!" I said. "Whoever is stealing equipment wants to keep it away from *other* players."

"Probably the good ones," said Nancy. "The best players all happen to be right-handed."

"Then the robber is probably left-handed," said Hannie.

The game was starting again. Nancy said she would peek at Kristy's notebook while we were playing. Then she would report back to us.

By the time the game ended, my team had won. And Nancy had important information.

"The players' section of the notebook is arranged alphabetically," said Nancy. "The pages that are missing go from M to W. The robber's last name probably begins with one of those letters."

"The criminal is not any of the kids whose statistics were changed," said Hannie. "Those numbers were made lower. The criminal would have made his or her own numbers higher."

"I noticed the other day that the new

numbers were written in with extra-dark pencil. And the eraser turned the page pink," I said.

"We are looking for a left-handed kid," said Hannie.

"Whose last name begins with a letter between M and W," said Nancy.

"The criminal uses a dark pencil with a pinkish eraser," I said.

Hmm. These were very interesting clues.

Ewww and Ouch

"Ewww!" cried Natalie.

We were at practice on Friday. Kristy was giving Natalie a turn at being catcher. Natalie flung the catcher's mitt across the field.

"What is wrong?" asked Kristy, running to her.

"Slime! Ewwy-gooey slime!" replied Natalie. She looked as though she were going to cry.

I ran over with Hannie and Nancy to check out the glove. Sure enough, there was Elmer's glue inside. Someone had

squeezed some of it into the fingers of the glove.

Natalie felt better when she found out what was on her fingers. But she was still shaken up. We were trying to calm her down when we heard another Krusher scream, "Ouch!"

It was Jake Kuhn. He is eight and a really nice kid. Poor Jake was lying in a heap across a pile of bats. He was holding his ankle. He was rocking and moaning. I was the first one to reach him.

"Let me help you take off your sneaker," I said.

While I was untying the laces, I saw something interesting. There was an old baseball card wrapped in plastic on the ground. As soon as Kristy came over to help with Jake, I slipped the card into my pocket.

I waved to Hannie and Nancy. It was time for another meeting.

"I do not understand how those bats fell down all at once," said Nancy. "I leaned them up against the wall just as carefully as I always do it. The bats should never have fallen down."

"Unless someone gave them a push," said Hannie.

"Look what I found," I said. I pulled the baseball card out of my pocket. We studied it together. It was a four-year-old card in excellent condition.

"It is probably part of a private collection," said Nancy.

"The criminal's private collection!" said Hannie.

"I bet he or she dropped it after pushing the bats down," I said.

"That was so mean," said Hannie. "It is one thing to put Elmer's glue on a ball or in a glove. That cannot hurt anyone. But it is another thing to make a kid fall over all those bats."

"You are right," I said. "But now we will catch that criminal for sure. We have another excellent clue to add to our list. We can be pretty sure that the criminal has a baseball card collection."

This was a very good day's work for the Three Musketeers Detective Agency.

Jake Kuhn's mom came to take him home. (Thank goodness he was not hurt too badly.) Natalie decided to sit out the practice. The rest of us played ball. But we did not play very well. It is hard to play ball with a criminal on the loose.

Kristy's Idea

Kristy plopped down on the grass after the game. She looked beat. We all fell down around her. We felt the same way.

"I think we need a break from practicing," she said. "I am giving everyone the weekend off. The next practice will be on Monday."

This was good news. But Kristy had more good news to tell us.

"I have been thinking about the state of our equipment," she said. "Most of it is either missing or in terrible shape. We need new equipment for our team."

"That will cost a lot of money," said Ricky. (My pretend husband is very practical.)

"I know that," replied Kristy. "And I have an idea about how we can raise the money we need. The Krushers will hold a toy sale."

"Cool!" I said. A toy sale would be fun.

"Kids can donate their used toys to me," continued Kristy. "The sale will be at my house a week from Saturday. I can advertise during the week. That way lots of kids will come and all the money will go toward buying new equipment for the Krushers."

Everyone liked Kristy's idea. Haley and Charlotte and Vanessa jumped up and led us in a cheer.

"Two, four, six, eight, who do we appreciate? Kristy! Kristy! Hooray!"

"Thanks, team," replied Kristy. "See you Monday. And remember, gather up those old toys. We need all we can get."

Mrs. Dawes came to pick up Nancy, Andrew, and me. When we got to the little house, we burst through the door and told Mommy our news about the sale.

"That is great," Mommy replied. "I will help you clean out your closets and play-room tomorrow."

Yikes. Kristy had not said anything about cleaning.

"I think I have some old toys lying around my room," I said. "We do not really have to go through the closets, do we?"

"You want to donate as many toys as you can, don't you?" asked Mommy.

"Well, yes. But isn't there another way? Besides cleaning up, I mean," I said.

Mommy shook her head.

"Tomorrow, bright and early," she said.

Good-bye, Toys

There was one thing I had to do on Saturday morning before going through my toys. I took out the telephone book and found a listing for "Baseball Cards — Sales." There was a shop in Stoneybrook called Stan's Souvenirs. I dialed the number and spoke to Stan himself.

"Um, I found a baseball card yesterday," I said. "I was wondering if it came from your shop."

I described the card. Stan did not remember it.

"Are you sure?" I asked. "It is part of an important criminal investigation."

Stan still did not remember it. I thanked him and hung up. I did not feel too bad. Maybe Stan did not remember the card. But it could still turn out to be a good clue.

I had breakfast with Mommy, Seth, and Andrew. I ate a bowl and a half of Krispy Krunchy cereal with blueberries on top. (I had the half a bowl for extra energy. I had the feeling getting rid of toys was going to be hard work.)

Seth went to his workshop. (He is a gigundoly good carpenter.) Andrew and I helped with the breakfast dishes.

Then Mommy said, "Karen, will you please get some rags? I will fill a bucket with soapy water. The last time I looked that playroom was pretty grimy."

Rags? Buckets? This sounded more like cleaning than I thought. I carried up a bag of rags and we got started.

Mommy held up a building set Andrew and I used to play with all the time.

"How about this toy? Can we sell it?" asked Mommy.

"I want to keep it," I said.

"Do you play with it?" asked Mommy.

"No," Andrew replied. "I forgot we had it."

"Karen, why do you want to keep it if you do not play with it anymore?" asked Mommy.

"I just like it," I said.

"Well, all right," sighed Mommy. She dusted it off and put it back on the shelf.

"How about this?" she asked. She held up an old cow puppet I had given Andrew for his birthday one year.

"It's Minnie-Moo!" said Andrew. "She used to moo when you squeezed her. But her mooer broke."

"Can we give her away?" asked Mommy.
Andrew nodded.

"Wait! We have to keep her," I said.

"She is Andrew's puppet," Mommy replied.

"But I gave Minnie-Moo to him. She

might not like going to a new home. She might get upset," I said.

"We have to give toys to Kristy," said Andrew. "She needs money to buy equipent."

"That's *equipment*," I said. "And I am sure she will get plenty of other toys."

"How about this old tea set, Karen? Grandma Packett gave you a beautiful new one," said Mommy.

"The new set is very nice. But I do not want to give away my old set," I replied.

"Please tell me why," said Mommy. "You never use it."

"It was my very first tea set. It has sentimetal value," I replied.

"That's *sentimental*," said Mommy. "And I think it is time to say good-bye to it. It is just collecting dust."

"I will dust it, then," I said.

I grabbed a rag and wiped every cup and saucer.

"I give up, Karen," said Mommy. She turned to Andrew.

"Andrew, how about this wind-up bear?" she asked.

"It does not wind up anymore," said Andrew.

"And this?" asked Mommy. She held up a jigsaw puzzle with great big pieces.

"It is for babies," said Andrew.

She held up one toy after another. Andrew was good about giving away his toys. I was having trouble parting with all but a few of mine. If they left it to me, Kristy would not even have enough money to buy a softball!

15

Just the Facts

Sunday morning is a day off for most people. But not for the members of the Three Musketeers Detective Agency. We could not rest. We had work to do.

Kristy was having her toy sale to buy new equipment for the Krushers next Saturday. If we did not solve the softball mystery, there would be no softball team to use the new equipment.

I called Nancy.

"Can you come over right away?" I asked.

Nancy said yes. She called Hannie. Before I knew it we were all up in my room. I closed the door for privacy.

I took out my magnifying glass in case we needed to use it. I handed out the detective's hats I had made the night before. I had written the initials T.M.D.A. on each one.

"The first thing we need to do is make a list of crimes committed against the Krushers," I said.

"I hope you have a lot of paper," said Hannie. "We have a long list of crimes to write down."

Here is the list we came up with:

CRIMES

PAGES M–W MISSING FROM KRISTY'S NOTEBOOK
TWO BATS MISSING
TWO LEFT-HAND CATCHER'S MITTS MISSING
TWO RIGHT-HAND BATTING GLOVES MISSING

STATISTICS ERASED, PHONY NUMBERS WRITTEN IN
NOTEBOOK
ELMER'S GLUE FOUND IN TWO CATCHER'S MITTS
BATS KNOCKED OVER TO TRIP JAKE

"We are dealing with a dangerous criminal here," I said.

"Now let's write down all the clues we have," said Nancy.

I took out a second sheet of paper and started writing:

CLUES

ONLY RIGHT-HAND EQUIPMENT MISSING. CRIMINAL
IS PROBABLY LEFT-HANDED.
BASEBALL CARD FOUND AT CRIME SCENE.
CRIMINAL IS PROBABLY A CARD COLLECTOR.
PLAYER STATISTICS LOWERED. CRIMINAL WOULD
NOT BE ONE OF THOSE PLAYERS.
M-W PLAYER PAGES MISSING. CRIMINAL'S LAST
NAME PROBABLY BEGINS WITH ONE OF THOSE LETTERS.
DARK WRITING AND PINK ERASER MARKS LEFT IN

70

NOTEBOOK. CRIMINAL USED A CHARCOAL PENCIL WITH A PINK ERASER.

"Now we need a list of suspects," said Nancy.

I hated to say what I was thinking. But a good detective needs to be ruthless.

"I think my brother, David Michael, is a suspect," I said. "He has not been allowed to come to some practices and he is very angry at Kristy for not taking his side."

"How about that Jack Darvin?" said Hannie. "He does not seem to like Kristy at all. He is always bossing her around."

"Mr. Benson will do anything to see that Marty does well on the team," said Nancy. "Marty's left-handed, by the way."

"Julian Spencer is left-handed, too. And his sister, Barbie, is pretty pushy," I said.

We talked about a few other kids, but found good reasons for ruling each one out. We were left with four main suspects. I wrote down their names:

SUSPECTS

DAVID MICHAEL
JACK DARVIN
ALBERT BENSON
BARBIE SPENCER

"We forgot to mention two other suspects," said Hannie. "Didn't you say that a couple of Bashers were spying on us?"

"You are right. I forgot about Jerry and Joanna," I said.

I added their names to the list. That made six suspects. Watch out, criminal, here we come!

Kristy's Toy Sale

We were back at practice on Monday. The criminal was back at work, too. There were several more reports of missing equipment. But the Three Musketeers did not uncover any other important clues. By the end of practice on Friday, we were stumped.

"See you tomorrow at the toy sale," called Hannie. She headed home with her brother, Linny.

On Saturday, I was up bright and early. My family had breakfast together. Mommy said she would drive Andrew and me to the big house for the toy sale when we finished.

"You hardly donated any toys, Karen," said Mommy. "Are you sure you do not want to give up the tea set? It would bring a good price to help buy equipment for your team."

I wanted to help the Krushers. But I wanted to keep my tea set more.

"I will think about it," I said.

I thought about it for two seconds and decided to keep my tea set. When it was time to go, though, I saw Mommy carrying it out to the car.

"No! No! You can take Minnie-Moo instead," I said.

"The tea set will get a better price. It is old. You do not use it. It is time to say good-bye," said Mommy.

"What if I want to have lots of friends over for tea? I might need it then," I said.

"I will give you my real tea cups if that happens," said Mommy.

I could see Mommy was not going to take no for an answer. I said good-bye to the pot first. Then to each cup. (There were six.) Then each saucer. (Six again.) Then I sang and acted out, "I'm a Little Teapot" until it was time to get in the car.

We arrived at the big house while Kristy was setting up for the sale. A few of her friends were helping out. Mommy and Andrew carried our carton of toys to one of the tables. I carried my tea set by itself. (I thought about hiding it, but I knew Mommy would notice it was missing.)

Kristy's friend Abby Stevenson came over to help us arrange and price our donations.

"This tea set is great," she said. "We will put a high price on it."

She made a tag and hung it on the teapot. She put the set at the center of the table. When the table was ready, Mommy took Andrew home, and I went to find Hannie and Nancy.

"Let's go check out the toys," said

Nancy. "I haven't decided whether to buy a few little ones, or one big one."

We circled the yard once. New kids kept arriving with more toys. So we went around again. Every so often I turned to see if my tea set was still on the table. It was.

While I was checking out my tea set, Barbie and Julian Spencer arrived. Barbie was wearing another cool outfit. Julian was tagging along behind, as usual. They showed Kristy their toys. I watched Barbie take an album from their carton. At first I thought it was a photograph album. Then I saw that it was an album that held cards. Baseball cards! I took a closer look.

"Hey, can I see that album?" I asked.

"Sure," replied Julian.

The baseball cards were arranged in alphabetical order by the players' names and also by year. There was one empty space in the book. It was the exact place where the mystery baseball card would go. Hmm.

"Thanks for bringing this great carton of

stuff," said Kristy. "If you give me your phone number, I will call you to pick up any toys we do not sell."

Barbie took a pencil out of her pocket. It had a dark charcoal point and a pink eraser! I noticed that she wrote with her right hand, not her left. But I already knew the reason for that.

Eureka! I had found our criminal!

Case Closed

"Explain this!" I said.

I reached into my pocket and pulled out the baseball card I had picked up on the field.

Barbie stood there with her mouth hanging open. Hannie and Nancy ran to see what was going on. Since Barbie was not saying anything, I decided to do the talking for her.

"The Three Musketeers Detective Agency has been hot on your trail," I said. "We know the changes in Kristy's book were

made with *that* pencil you are holding in your hand!"

I pointed to the pencil.

"The stolen equipment was for right-handed players only. Not for left-handed players like *that* player next to you!" I said. I pointed to Julian.

"You were committing all the crimes against the Krushers for Julian's sake, weren't you?" I said.

"Huh?" said Julian.

He looked up at his sister and she poured out her story.

"Karen is right. I admit everything," she said. "I wanted my brother to look extra good on the softball field. I thought if I messed things up for the good players, Julian would look better. I thought that would help him fit in and make new friends more quickly."

"So that was why you stole right-hand equipment. And it is why you put glue in the catcher's mitts," said Nancy.

"And that is why you lowered the statistics in the player book. And why you tripped Jake," said Hannie. "You are lucky he did not get hurt badly."

"I am sorry," said Barbie. "I never wanted to hurt anyone. I just wanted to help my brother."

"This was not the way to do it," said Kristy.

We left Kristy to deal with Barbie. The Three Musketeers had done their job. Our case was closed.

It was time to celebrate. It was time to buy some toys! I looked over at Abby's table.

"I wonder if Mommy would be mad at me if I bought back my tea set," I said.

Hannie and Nancy looked at each other.

"I would not do that if I were you," said Hannie.

"Hey, Karen. I think I hear Ricky calling you. He probably wants to hear about the case," said Nancy.

"Where is he? I did not hear him calling," I replied.

"He is over there," said Hannie, pointing toward the house. "You better go find him. We will wait here for you."

I went to look for Ricky. I did not find him. When I came back Hannie and Nancy were each holding one handle of a shopping bag.

"What did you buy?" I asked.

"A tea set," said Hannie.

"*Your* tea set," said Nancy. "Hannie and I chipped in and bought it together. I will keep it at my house. That way it will always be next door to the little house. You can play with it whenever you want."

"Thank you. You are the greatest!" I said.

"One for all and all for one!" the Three Musketeers said together.

We got busy buying toys. I bought lots of good things for myself. And I bought a toy for Hannie and one for Nancy, too. I even bought a toy for David Michael. (I felt bad about calling him a prime suspect.)

By the time Mommy came to pick me up,

my money was gone and my arms were full.

"Look what I got, Mommy. More toys!" I said.

Mommy groaned. A big grin spread across my face.

Welcome Back, Ms. Colman

Sunday was a happy day. And a busy one! I was happy because the mystery was solved. But that was not the only reason. Ms. Colman was coming back to school on Monday. For real this time.

That is why I was busy. Mommy and I were making cupcakes again for the party. (I had saved the cards I made before.)

Before I knew it, Sunday was gone and it was Monday — party day! Nancy and I raced to Mr. Berger's room to drop off our party things. Then we headed for our room.

We were the first ones there. Except for Ms. Colman. She was sitting at her desk as if she had never been gone. Nancy and I burst through the door.

"Welcome back, Ms. Colman!" I shouted.

(Ms. Colman usually reminds me to use my indoor voice when I shout in class. But she did not say anything this time. She knew it was a special occasion.)

Ms. Colman put one arm around Nancy and one around me.

"Thank you for that welcome, girls," she said. "I am happy to be back. I missed you."

"We missed you, too," I replied.

"Even though Mrs. Hoffman was nice," added Nancy.

"Mrs. Hoffman told me she enjoyed being your teacher very much," said Ms. Colman.

I was glad to hear that. I was glad we were giving *both* our teachers a surprise party.

The other kids were coming in. It was

time to start the day. Guess who got to take attendance. Me! Not one kid was absent.

We told Ms. Colman about the things we had been doing with Mrs. Hoffman. She told us all about Jane. She even passed around baby pictures. Jane was gigundoly cute. And in one picture she was lying on the blanket I had made! I felt very proud.

Ms. Colman picked up with our schoolwork right where Mrs. Hoffman had left off. We took our lunch and recess break. Then, at two o'clock sharp, there was a knock on our classroom door. It was Mr. Berger. He was right on schedule.

"I believe you left a few things in my room," he said.

Five of us went next door to get our party things. When we returned, the class shouted, "Surprise, Ms. Colman! Welcome back!"

I handed her the card I had made. (Everyone had signed it.)

"This is a wonderful surprise!" replied Ms. Colman with a big smile. "Thank you very much."

Then there was another knock at the door. It was Mrs. Hoffman. As soon as she walked in, the kids all shouted, "Surprise, Mrs. Hoffman!"

I handed her the other card.

"I thought I was here to help with Ms. Colman's party," said Mrs. Hoffman. She was smiling, too.

"We decided you should have a party, too, because you have been such a good substitute teacher," I replied.

"You are very thoughtful," said Mrs. Hoffman. "Thank you."

The party was lots of fun. We ate, sang songs, and played games. We were sad when it was time for Mrs. Hoffman to go. But we knew we would see her again on days when Ms. Colman could not come to school.

After the party, we cleaned up and put

our room back in order. My worries were finally over. My beloved teacher, Ms. Colman, had really and truly returned.

No matter how much I like anyone else, no one can take her place.

19

A Special Visitor

Friday came fast. It was our last day of school before summer vacation.

After morning announcements and attendance, which was taken by Ricky, Ms. Colman looked up at the door.

"A special visitor has just arrived," she said. "Really there are two special visitors."

She waved them inside. Ms. Colman's husband, Mr. Simmons, walked in carrying their baby, Jane, in his arms.

"Ooh, she is so cute!" I said.

I jumped up to see her face.

"You may sit down, Karen," said Ms. Colman. "We will bring Jane around so everyone can see her."

Ms. Colman and Mr. Simmons walked by my row first.

"Hi, Mr. Simmons!" I said. "Jane is even cuter than in the pictures we saw."

(I have met Mr. Simmons lots of times before. I was even a flower girl at Ms. Colman's and Mr. Simmons's wedding.)

"Thank you, Karen. She is very special to us," Mr. Simmons replied.

Jane was dressed in pink. She was wide awake and cooing. She had soft brown skin, curly black hair, and big, dark, sparkly eyes.

"Kootchy-kootchy-koo!" called Bobby.

He was being silly. But Jane liked it. She started to laugh.

"Jane is three months old now," said Ms. Colman. "She sleeps through the night. She likes to wiggle her body and kick her feet. And she already loves books."

"Maybe you would like to take turns

reading to her," said Mr. Simmons.

He brought out a book called *Baby's Mother Goose Rhymes.*

"Who would like to begin?" asked Ms. Colman.

My hand shot up first.

"We marked off some of her favorite rhymes," said Mr. Simmons.

Crash! Wah-wah!

Someone behind me had dropped something that made a loud noise. It must have scared Jane. She went from being a happy, smiling baby to a scared and crying one.

Ms. Colman took Jane in her arms and rocked her while Mr. Simmons stroked her head. I found a marker in the book and began to read.

"Pat-a-cake, pat-a-cake, baker's man.
Bake me a cake as fast as you can."

Jane stopped crying and looked at me. I continued reading.

"Pat it and prick it, and mark it with B,
Put it in the oven for baby and me."

By the time I finished, Jane was smiling

again. Ms. Colman and Mr. Simmons were smiling, too.

"Thank you, Karen," said Ms. Colman.

"You are welcome," I said.

I passed the book to Ricky so he could read some more rhymes.

Play Ball!

On Saturday we played the first official softball game of the season. It was the Krushers against the Bashers.

Kristy had decided not to cut any players from our big team after all. She had decided everyone who wanted to play should have a chance. That meant the field was crowded. But no one seemed to mind.

The toy sale had been a big success. By the time it was over, Kristy was able to buy almost every piece of equipment we needed.

Barbie bought the rest of the equipment for us with her own money. It was her way of apologizing to the team. She presented the equipment at the game and apologized in person.

"I hope none of you are angry at Julian," she said. "He had nothing to do with what I did."

We were not one bit angry at Julian. And we had already forgiven Barbie. We could tell she was sorry for what she did. She was being very nice and helpful, too. She even brought refreshments for the team.

"It is almost time for the game to begin," said Kristy. "How about a team cheer?"

Vanessa and Haley and Charlotte jumped up and waved their pompoms in the air.

"Come on, team!" they shouted. "Give us K-R-U!"

"K-R-U!" the team shouted back.

"Give us S-H-E!" shouted the cheer-leaders.

"S-H-E!" we shouted back.

"We'll give you an R! We'll give you an

S! Then what will you get?" shouted our cheerleaders.

"KRUSHERS!" we replied.

Kristy and Bart gave each other the thumbs-up sign.

"Play ball!" they called.

The Krushers were first at bat. And I was first up for the Krushers. I waved to Mommy and Seth. They were sitting on a blanket on the grass. Then I waved to my big-house family. They were on beach chairs at the other side of the field.

I walked up to home plate. The first ball came fast. Whoosh! I swung at it and missed. Strike one.

The second ball fooled me. It seemed to be coming straight, then it curved. Whoosh! I missed again. Strike two.

"Take it easy, Karen," called Kristy. "You can hit that ball. I know you can."

Kids were shouting all around me. I heard Hannie's voice. And Nancy's. I heard David Michael and Andrew and Ricky. I was starting to get nervous. I could not let everyone down.

The ball came flying toward me. Crack! I hit the ball. I ran to first base. Then I ran to second. I saw the ball heading toward third so I stayed where I was.

I had hit a double. I jumped up and down. I shouted, "Yippee!"

Julian was up next.

"Come on, Julian! Hit me home!" I called.

"Go, Julian, go!" called Barbie.

I watched the ball fly though the air. I heard the crack of the bat as it hit the ball. Then I was running toward third and watching the ball at the same time. It went over the wall of the playground. I headed for home plate. Julian had hit a home run!

We all ran to congratulate him. He looked proud. Barbie looked proud, too. It turned out she did not have to do anything to make her little brother shine on the team. He was able to do it all by himself.

The score at the end of the game was close: Krushers 5, and Bashers 6. We all had fun. And we all walked away friends. It was a great start to our Stoneybrook summer.

L. GODWIN

About the Author

ANN M. MARTIN lives in New York City and loves animals, especially cats. She has two cats of her own, Gussie and Woody.

Other books by Ann M. Martin that you might enjoy are *Stage Fright*; *Me and Katie (the Pest)*; and the books in *The Baby-sitters Club* series.

Ann likes ice cream and *I Love Lucy*. And she has her own little sister, whose name is Jane.

Little Sister

Don't miss #75

KAREN'S COUNTY FAIR

"Entering an animal in a contest is a serious project, Karen," said Mrs. Stone. "It takes a lot of time and effort."

Kristy reminded me about the livestock contest we saw on TV. "Those kids spent hours every day with their animals. They fed them, groomed them, and taught them how to behave."

"I can spend hours each day with Ollie," I said.

"Well, all right, Karen," Mrs. Stone finally said. "I see you are determined. But this means you will be in a group by yourself."

"That is all right," I said. I was thrilled. I ran outside to give my lamb a hug. "Ollie," I whispered. "We are going to win the blue ribbon."

LITTLE ■ APPLE®

BABYSITTERS

Little Sister™

by Ann M. Martin,
author of The Baby-sitters Club®

More Titles... ➡

Say "cheese," Little Sister!

BABY·SITTERS ™

Little Sister
Photo Scrapbook
Book and Camera Package

Smile for the camera—and then save all your
pictures in a cool scrapbook filled with special
frames and fill-ins. Now you can make your very
own photo-guide to family, friends, school, and
holidays. Plus—the 110-mm camera is reusable,
so you can take all the photographs you want!

Available this summer at a bookstore near you.